RRRALPH

Lois Ehlert

Beach Lane Books • New York London Toronto Sydney

I bet you
won't believe me,
but our dog
can talk.

I found out
when we first
brought him home
and I asked:

What's your name?

We built
a house for him
and a really
high fence
all around
our backyard.

Hey, Ralph!
Where are you?

Ralph likes to chase the backyard birds. I always tell him no, but he never listens.

Ralph,
what's on that tree?

I think Ralph
needs a long walk
in the woods.

How's the path feel on your paws, Ralph?

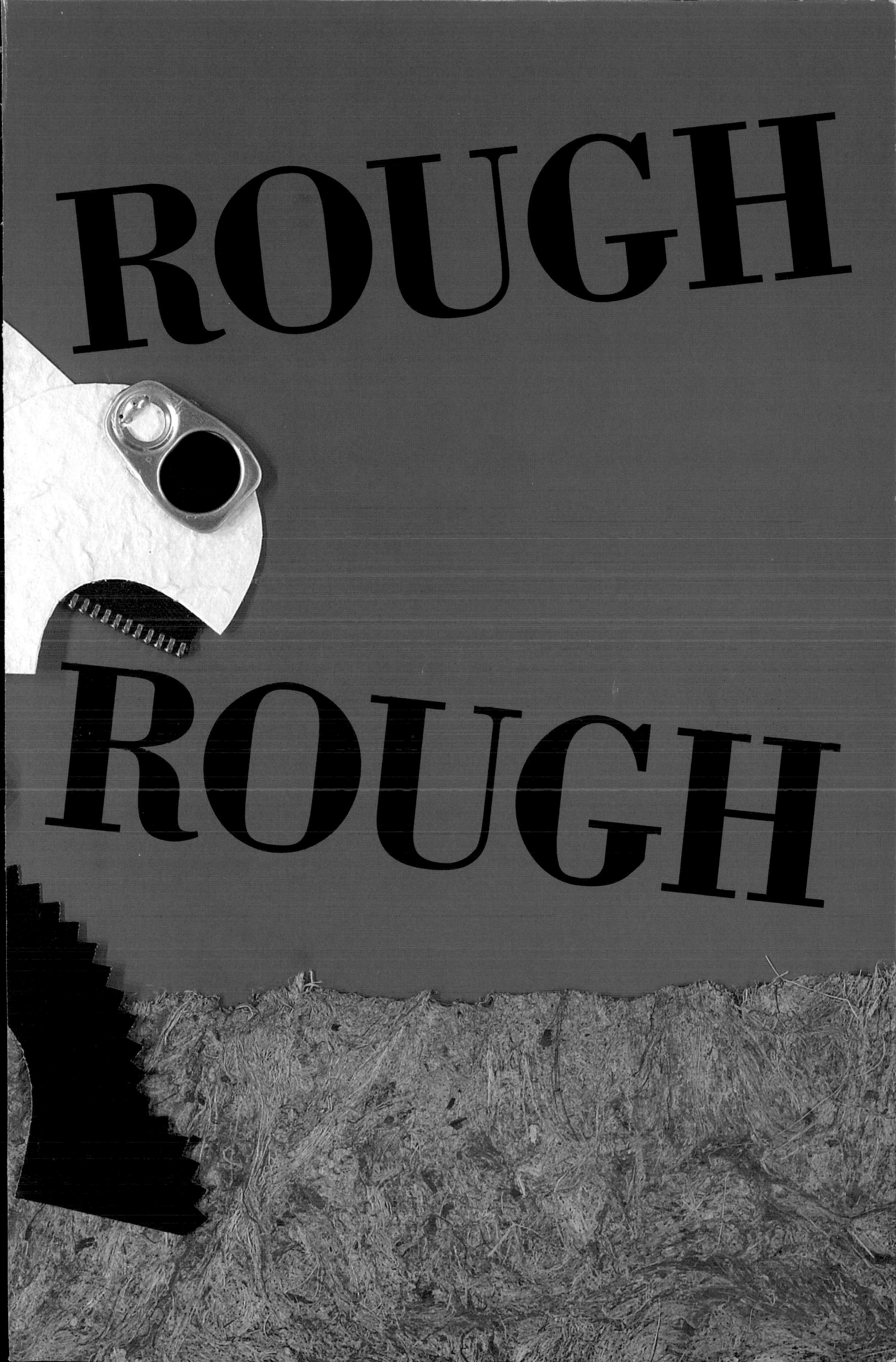

ROUGH

ROUGH

So we race
back home on the
soft grass.
As I latch the fence
gate, we hear a howl.

What's
that,
Ralph?

WOLF!

Don't be scared,
Ralph!
He can't get in.
But want to come
into the house
with me?

YEP

YEP

YEP

Oh, Ralph,
isn't it great
to have a friend?

Good night,
sleepyhead.
Talk to you
tomorrow!

Author's Note

This book was inspired by jokes that my brother, Dick Ehlert, told to his grandchildren.

In real life, the wild backyard intruder would more likely have been a coyote, not a wolf, because coyotes are much more prevalent in suburban habitats.

Coyotes, wolves, and dogs are all related. Can these animals talk to us? You decide.

BEACH LANE BOOKS
An imprint of Simon & Schuster Children's Publishing Division
1230 Avenue of the Americas, New York, New York 10020
Copyright © 2011 by Lois Ehlert
All rights reserved, including the right of reproduction in whole or in part in any form.
BEACH LANE BOOKS is a trademark of Simon & Schuster, Inc.
For information about special discounts for bulk purchases,
please contact Simon & Schuster Special Sales at 1-866-506-1949
or business@simonandschuster.com.
The Simon & Schuster Speakers Bureau can bring authors to your live event. For more
information or to book an event, contact the Simon & Schuster Speakers Bureau
at 1-866-248-3049 or visit our website at www.simonspeakers.com.
The text for this book is set in Century Expanded and Bodoni Bold.
The illustrations for this book were made from zippers, wood, buttons, twine, metal, tree bark,
screws, hand-painted and handmade papers, and textile fragments.
Manufactured in China
0411 SCP

10 9 8 7 6 5 4 3 2
Library of Congress Cataloging-in-Publication Data
Ehlert, Lois.
Rrralph / Lois Ehlert. — 1st ed.
p. cm.
Summary: The narrator describes discovering how Ralph the dog can talk,
appropriately saying words such as "roof," "rough," "bark," and "wolf."
ISBN 978-1-4424-1305-4 (hardcover)
[1. Dogs—Fiction. 2. Humorous stories.] I. Title. II. Title: Ralph.
PZ7.E3225Rr 2011
[E]—dc22
2010006866